WHAT TO DO WHEN YOU PANIC

A Kid's Guide to Transforming Panic Into Personal Power

by **Lenka Glassman, PsyD**

illustrated by
Janet McDonnell

Magination Press • Washington, DC
American Psychological Association

**To Emma & Ella: you are so loved, no matter what!
To any kid who's felt powerless about panic: you are strong,
capable, and clever enough to overcome it. One day, this experience
will fuel your superpowers—*LG***

Text copyright © 2025 by Lenka Glassman. Illustrations copyright © 2025 by Janet McDonnell. Published in 2025 by Magination Press, an imprint of the American Psychological Association. All rights reserved. Except as permitted under the United States Copyright Act of 1976, no part of this publication may be reproduced or distributed in any form or by any means, or stored in a database or retrieval system, without the prior written permission of the publisher. *What to Do When You Panic* is part of the Magination Press What-to-Do Guides for Kids® series, a registered trademark of the American Psychological Association.

Magination Press, Books for Kids From the American Psychological Association
maginationpress.org

Distributed by Lerner Publisher Services
lernerbooks.com

Book design by Christina Gaugler
Printed by Worzalla, Stevens Point, WI

Library of Congress Cataloging-in-Publication Data

Names: Glassman, Lenka, author. | McDonnell, Janet, 1962- illustrator. Title: What to do when you panic: a kid's guide to transforming panic into personal power/by Lenka Glassman; illustrated by Janet McDonnell.

Description: Washington, DC: Magination Press, [2025] | Series: What-to-do guides for kids series Audience term: Children | Audience term: School children | Summary: "An interactive self-help book designed to help kids overwhelmed with panicky feelings and stress, using scientifically proven techniques most often used by psychologists and school counselors"—Provided by publisher.

Identifiers: LCCN 2024032966 (print) | LCCN 2024032967 (ebook) | ISBN 9781433844843 (paperback) | ISBN 9781433845130 (ebook)

Subjects: LCSH: Fear—Juvenile literature. | Panic attacks—Juvenile literature. | Stress (Psychology)—Juvenile literature.

Classification: LCC BF723.F4 G53 2025 (print) | LCC BF723.F4 (ebook) | DDC 155.4/1246—dc23/eng/20240807
LC record available at https://lccn.loc.gov/2024032966
LC ebook record available at https://lccn.loc.gov/2024032967

Manufactured in the United States of America
10 9 8 7 6 5 4 3 2

CONTENTS

NOTE TO PARENTS & CAREGIVERS

Picture this: you're dropped into a fairy tale and suddenly come face to face with a big bad werewolf. You don't know how you got there, and can't see a way out. That's what panic feels like for our kids.

The truth is, panic isn't extraordinary, but the kids who face it **ARE**. They have an innate strength and tenacity that is inspiring. But panic has covered it up and stopped them from facing life's challenges with the flexibility and grit that you know they possess.

When our kids panic, the sensations of fear in their body are all consuming. They know something feels terribly wrong but might not have the words to explain what is happening. They are overwhelmed by their thoughts, impulses, and emotions, and feel certain that something dreadful is about to happen. This might look like your child asking a ton of "what ifs," avoiding going to school, asking the same questions over and over, frequent anger and tears, a sick tummy, or not wanting to speak. Everything inside them is telling them something isn't right, so us telling them that there is nothing to panic about can leave them feeling alone and filled with self-doubt. Even worse, panic is tricky—the very things your instincts are guiding you to do can actually make your child's fear grow bigger and their belief in themselves get smaller.

In this workbook, your child will find simple, workable strategies to overcome panic and regain their confidence. Each chapter is packed with the very best, science-backed, experience-tested, parent-approved tools to help your child find stillness in their body, develop a "can do" mindset, face their fears, and build a solid sense of self-worth. Of course, I've sprinkled in just the right amount of **MAGIC** and fun to keep your child engaged and inspired. This book will work best if you take it slowly, together—don't rush through it just to get to the end. Encourage your child to take it one chapter at a time, practicing the strategies in each before moving on.

It's worth noting that some kids who struggle with panic go on to develop an anxiety disorder (like panic disorder) in their teens or young adulthood. Helping your child conquer their panic **NOW** can interrupt or even prevent this cycle of fear and avoidance from taking hold.

The bottom line is this: helping your child transform their relationship with panic early on sets them up for a healthier relationship with stress in the future.

Trust yourself, and remember that an important part of your child's emotional health is their relationship with **YOU**. Use this book to connect with them as they build resilience, cheer them on as they face their fears, and celebrate with them as they break free from panic. There is nothing more magical than witnessing your child re-discover their own strength. They are lucky to have you, and by supporting them on this journey you are setting them up for long-term well-being and confidence.

CHAPTER 1

Meet Panic

You are moments away from walking into a birthday party, feeling excited and ready for the fun. Out of nowhere, a huge wave of fear washes over you. You feel frozen in place, like you can't move another inch. Every part of your body is shouting:

"**STOP!** Don't go in! You can't do this!"

The strange thing is, you don't see any signs of danger. In fact, everything around you looks perfectly ordinary. Still…you can't shake the sense of overwhelming dread.

This feeling is called panic. And you probably already know it's no fairy tale. It can make you feel like you're trapped under a spell of fear, with no way out.

Panic instantly makes you feel overwhelmingly scared, and convinces you that something terrible is about to happen. These big feelings can make you want to stop in your tracks, get away, or avoid what's scaring you altogether. When you're panicked, you might act in ways that are unusual for you (like crying or shouting) because you'll do just about anything to make the feelings **STOP**. It truly **SEEMS** like you're fighting for your life.

Luckily, panic doesn't stay long. Just when you feel like giving up the fight, your fear fades away. Panic gets tired, shrinks down, and just leaves.

But… panic is quick and mighty. The experience feels so intense because it's a natural reaction in your body that's meant to keep you safe when you're facing real danger!

The trouble is, panic can show up even when there is NO danger at all.

This is exactly what happened to Sam just as he was about to play his first song at a piano recital. He had worked hard, and felt totally ready! But in an instant, his whole body froze up. His heart raced and his mind was scrambling to remember what he had practiced.

Have you ever felt something like this? Maybe when you're meeting new friends or trying something for the first time? Let your mind travel back to one of those moments and **draw** what that felt like. You can draw yourself in that situation, or something that reminds you of that moment.

Feelings of panic aren't unusual—most kids experience them at one point or another. Sometimes panic sneaks up unexpectedly and you're not even sure why. Other times it's obvious what caused it, like facing a big challenge.

Some common things that make kids panic include:

- Being away from your parents

- Sleeping or being alone in a dark room

- New or scary situations (like getting vaccines, traveling on a plane, performing on stage, or the first day of school)

- Not being prepared for an activity (like not having practiced for piano)

- Specific animals like snakes, spiders, dogs, or sharks

- Places where there are a lot of people, like school or a theme park

- Feeling big and difficult emotions

- Forgetting something important like your homework or glasses

What are some things that make your panic appear? Maybe it's some of the above, or maybe it's totally different.

____

____

____

For some kids, moments of panic start to happen over and over, making it hard to do some of the things you have to do, like going to school, and even things you love to do, like spending time with friends. You might begin avoiding these activities altogether, which only makes your panic grow **BIGGER** and your life feel smaller. Worst of all, panic can trick you into believing that you aren't strong enough to handle life's challenges. Does this story sound like yours?

The good news is, you are much stronger than panic, and getting free from it is way **SIMPLE**. You see, panic isn't as powerful as it pretends to be—it only has one trick up its sleeve, and it has some big-time weaknesses.

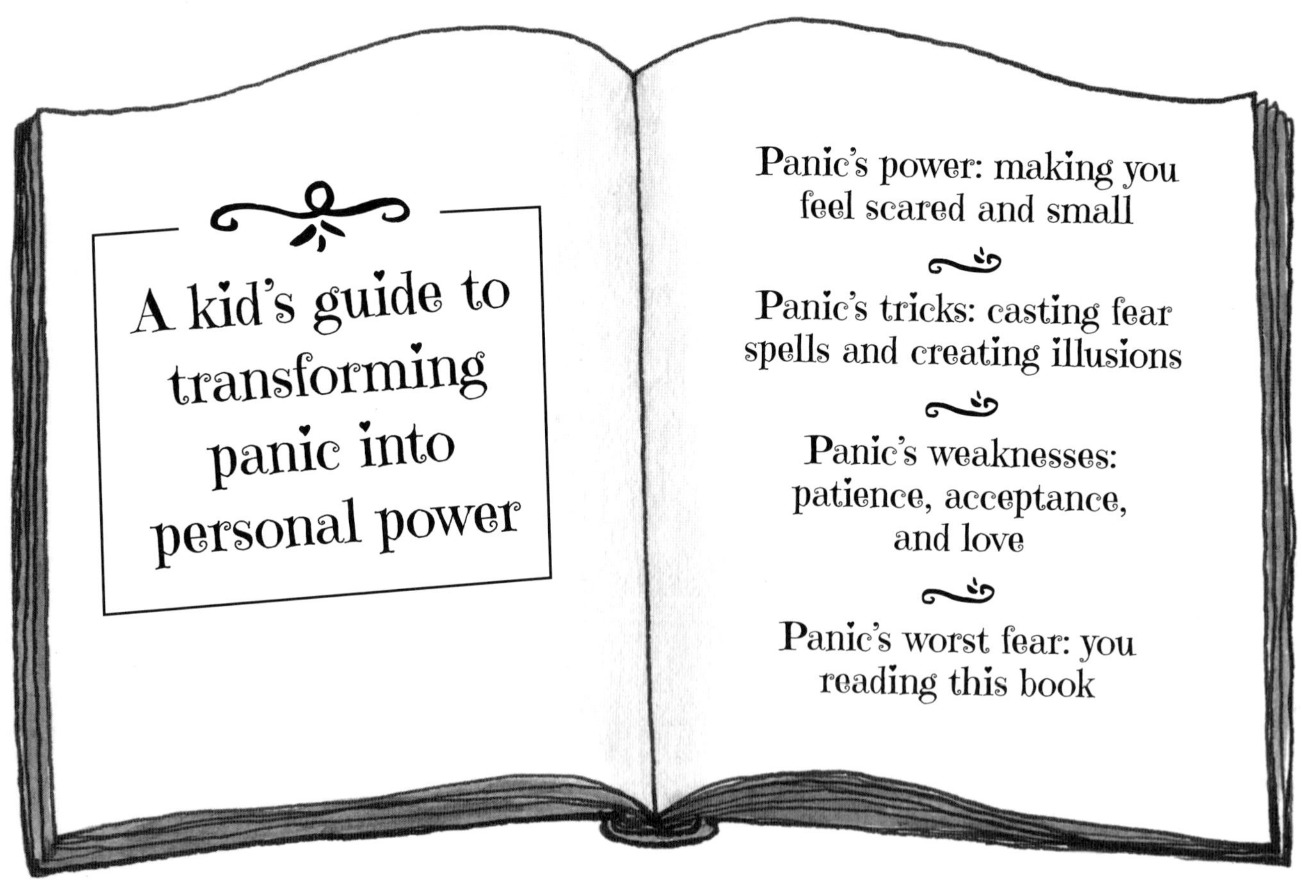

That's right. Panic tricks you into feeling scared because it's excellent at creating the **ILLUSION** of danger. Like casting a spell of fear, panic makes your mind and body feel terrified, even when you are completely 100% **SAFE**. It makes you feel like you **CAN'T**, even though you totally **CAN**.

Are you ready to turn your fear into courage? This book will help you take away panic's only powers and use all of its weaknesses to your advantage. By the time you're finished, you'll know exactly how to undo a fear spell, master some magic of your own, and find your confidence. Panic will have zero power in your life.

Let's do this!

CHAPTER 2

Once Upon a Time... Panic Was Great!

Is that a mistake? Nope. It's true. A long, long time ago (when humans still lived in caves and had to fight daily for food, shelter, and survival), the human mind and body figured out how to help us survive the serious and immediate danger that was all around us.

Panic helped humans freeze perfectly still when a sabretooth tiger was close by, or fight with all their might when they were attacked by a wild bear, or run faster than lightning when they had to get themselves to safety in a big storm.

In those split-second moments, humans needed to act powerfully and right away, without stopping to think about their best option or arguing with their predators.

Can you imagine your ancestors in front of a bear who's running straight at them, pausing to say:

Or stopping to think :

Exactly. Panic was lifesaving, and speed was its superpower.

So just how does panic help us fight, escape, or freeze?

It's all about our nervous system, which includes our brain, spinal cord, and nerves that run throughout our body. The brain is our control center, and the spinal cord is the main highway on which messages travel between our brain and body.

There are two parts of this system: the **ACTIVATING** system, which helps us react quickly to scary or stressful events, and the **CALMING** system, which helps us relax and restore. Our activating and calming systems work together, like good friends, to keep us in balance.

What turns on these systems? Our brain of course! Our brain has several different parts, each with its own set of jobs.

When we are in a life-threatening emergency, the "survival" and "feeling" parts spring into action. They send alarm signals through our **ACTIVATING** system to ready our body to fight, freeze, or escape.

At the same time, our "thinking brain," which controls decision-making, problem-solving, and thoughtfulness, gets very quiet, and our **CALMING** system steps out of the way. Within seconds, our activating system jumps into overdrive, while our calming system takes a backseat.

Don't worry, these two systems go back to being true partners once the danger is gone.

In emergencies, panic goes right! Imagine a fairy tale hero who thinks he's finally defeated the villain and saved his friends...and then he sees the villain's whole crew coming straight at him!

In an instant, he's cornered, surrounded, and way outnumbered. Enter panic!

His brain sends emergency signals to his body to ready him to fight (or run for his life).

His mind is laser-focused on surviving, so he doesn't get distracted by anything that could slow him down, like the sound of the villain's creepy voice or trying to figure out how they could have gotten away in the first place.

His breathing gets faster so his body can take in extra oxygen, which makes him more powerful. His heartbeat is racing, sending energy to his arms and legs so he can fight harder, fly faster, and leap higher.

See? Our panic system is so great! Can you think of a time when your mind and body worked together at lightning speed to keep you safe at just the right time?

► Riding your skateboard and seeing a biker come straight towards you out of the corner of your eye, and swerving out of the way just in time?

► Slipping on an icy spot on your way to school and somehow being able to stay on your feet?

► Seeing your best friend crossing the street in front of you and pulling them back to the sidewalk just before a car comes around the corner?

Draw or write about a time that panic kept you safe!

CHAPTER 3

Panic Is Trying to Find Its Place

Fast forward to right now, today. We humans are at the top of the food chain. Most of us don't face life-threatening danger that often. Yet panic hasn't really…evolved along with us.

Panic is incredibly fast and strong, which was useful when big danger lurked behind every corner. But panic isn't very accurate. Sometimes it can't tell the difference between true danger and everyday little stresses that you experience (like forgetting your homework). This means that panic can show up even if you're in a perfectly safe situation. It overreacts.

That. Is. A. Big. Problem.

Valentina was walking into class and realized she'd forgotten her homework. Everyone else was getting their worksheet out of their bag, and she didn't have hers. Suddenly her stomach dropped, her arms and legs started shaking, her breathing got faster, and she felt like she might faint! It was almost like she was caught under a spell of fear!

Her panic system reacted instantly, the same way it would to *real life-threatening danger.*

Valentina realizes she forgot her homework.

She feels fear & dread, her heart beats faster, and her thoughts start racing. Her brain goes on high alert, sending danger signals to the rest of her body.

Survival reflexes kick in! Valentina's mind is laser focused on surviving and nothing else (this makes it hard to pay attention to what the teacher is saying, or what she can actually do about her missing homework).

Her breathing gets fast, and because she isn't running for her life, this just makes her feel like she can't get enough air.

Energy flows away from body parts that aren't needed in a fight (like her stomach), making her feel...queasy.

Energy flows towards her arms and legs, powering them up. Since she isn't running or fighting, it just makes her feel shaky, sweaty, and tense.

See how panic can make danger feel so real, even when it's not? That's why the **illusion works!**

Circle the moments that are truly dangerous, and cross out the moments that feel awful but aren't life-threatening.

A gorilla escaping the enclosure at the zoo and running after you.

Showing up to English class unprepared for the quiz.

Realizing you took your sibling's backpack to school instead of your own.

Sleeping in your room with the lights off.

Getting stung by a bee when you are allergic to bee stings.

Arriving at a sleepover and realizing your closest friend won't be there.

Crossing the road and seeing a car running a red light and racing your way.

You might be thinking, why do I panic more often than my friends or siblings?

Some brains are just more fear sensitive than others. Some kids are taller, or faster, or bigger, or better at sports. Others are creative, have an eye for style, and are great at art. Some kids love music and some love books. Some kids like watching scary movies and some don't. And some kids have brains with a more active panic system. No one thing is good or bad; it just is.

Catching Your Panic

To get free from panic, first you have to learn to catch it when it shows up, and to step back from the feelings it creates.

The faster you notice your panic, the more confidently you can respond to its tricks. The more distance you can get from it, the more easily you'll see through its illusions. To do this, you can learn to **spot it and name it.**

Spotting panic and its illusion of danger is important. You might be saying "I know when I'm scared!" But panic can be tricky; sometimes it shows up in different ways. Panic can affect how your body feels, what your mind thinks, and even what you do.

Knowing ahead of time exactly how panic shows up for **YOU** can help you identify it quickly when it strikes. It's like having magic magnifying glass that allows you to recognize that your panic is overreacting before you're caught in a fear spell. You might still feel uncomfortable (no one likes sweating in the middle of class), but you won't feel as stuck and afraid.

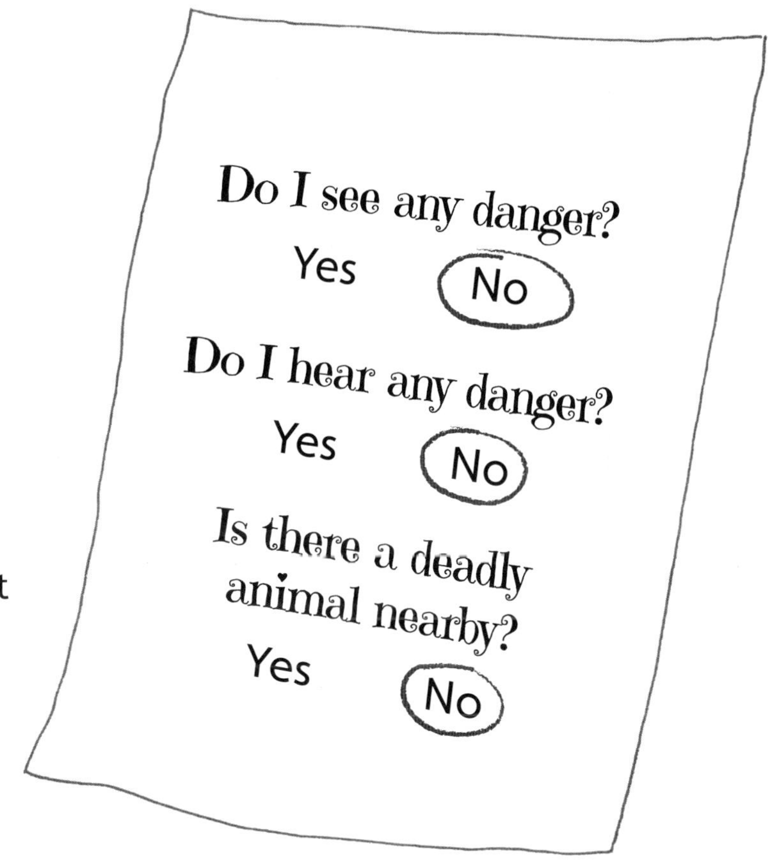

Do any of these sound familiar? Circle each experience that you've noticed in yourself when you panic.

Body

Feeling dizzy or light-headed

Nausea or stomach pain

Feeling like it is hard to breathe

Heartbeat racing

Your body feeling hot or cold

Breathing too quickly or too shallowly

Tingling or shaking in your arms, hands, or legs

Mind

Fear that you're out of control or going crazy

Racing worry thoughts like: "What if something bad happens?" or "I can't handle this!"

Feeling like things aren't real or like you're in a dream

Actions

A strong urge to get away, fight, or avoid something completely

Crying, shouting, shutting down, or feeling like you aren't able to speak

Draw the signs of your own panic. It's like taking a mental picture to help your brain spot panic easily. You can even draw a magic magnifying glass!

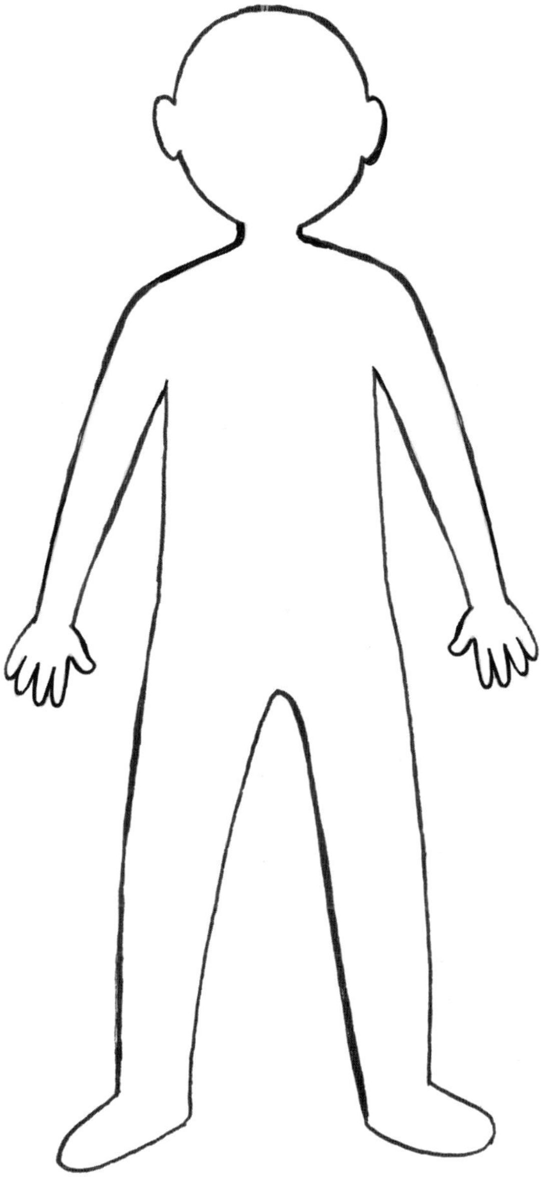

After you learn to spot panic when it shows up, give your panic a name and pretend like it has a life of its own. Imagine that it's a separate being with its own voice and viewpoint. This helps you see it as something separate from you, instead of feeling like you and your panic are one and the same.

Then you can get some distance, see things more clearly, and turn your thinking brain on so you feel less afraid.

The name can be something serious or something funny! Like:

- Smelly Banana
- Firefly
- T-Rex
- Shadow Spider
- Herbert Sherbert
- Batty Bat

Sam named his panic **"Wolfie"** because he saw it as strong, scary, and growly. Emma's panic reminded her of a giant, fiery dragon, so she named her panic **"Dragon."** While Valentina named her panic **"Scary Fairy"** because, well, it always seemed to flutter around her at the worst possible time.

The name of my panic is: _______________________________

____

Because it is: _______________________________

____

Once your panic has a name, picturing and drawing what it looks like can help you see its true form. Imagine that you have a magic mirror that allows you to see your panic for what it really IS instead of what it WANTS you to see.

When Emma's panic tried to show up before her dance class, she imagined it as a little dragon buzzing around her, trying to get in her way.

Draw your panic, just how you picture it. Imagine you have a
magic mirror that helps you see panic's true form.

When you take a step back from your panic, and see it more clearly, you might see other things in a different way too. Imagine that the magic mirror allows you to see yourself from a wider view. It shows you that, in the big picture of your life, YOU are the hero and panic is just one of your quirky sidekicks.

What are some other parts of you? Circle some that sound like you, and add your own!

a student

a big brother

a hockey player

a math wiz

a performer

a poet

a sister

a daughter

CHAPTER 5

Breaking a Fear Spell

Panic has only one power: to make you feel small and terrified. It uses all sorts of tricks and illusions to accomplish this. The ultimate key to undoing panic's fear spell is something you might not expect.

You **CAN'T** fight off, outrun, or avoid panic. In fact, if you try to do these things, the fear spell you're under only gets stronger, and lasts longer.

You **CAN** learn to respond to panic differently—in ways that trick it into believing that you aren't one bit afraid. When panic tries to scare you, welcome it with curiosity instead of fear. When it tries to push you into a struggle, treat it with love instead of anger. When it tries to pull you away, greet it with compassion.

Imagine this: Panic is knocking on your door, ready to scare you. Instead of locking the door to shut panic out, pretending you aren't home, or shouting at it to go away, you do something surprising. You open the door, welcome it in, invite it to sit down, and serve it a magic mug of hot chocolate.

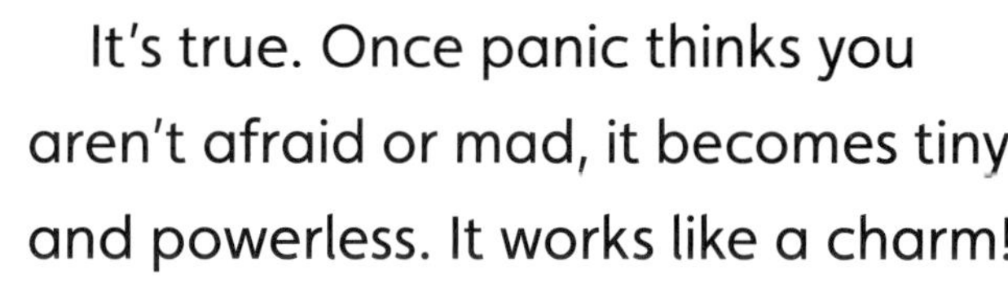

It's true. Once panic thinks you aren't afraid or mad, it becomes tiny and powerless. It works like a charm!

Over time, with practice, this changes the way your brain responds to stressful situations in the first place, and your fear fades away on its own.

After you welcome panic in, you have to accept it. **Accepting panic** means you'll treat it as if you're completely fine with it being there. Like you aren't even bothered. You let it stay with you without trying to change it or make it go away. If you accept panic and allow it to be there, it thinks you aren't afraid and just…gives up. Magical right?

But this can be tricky! It's hard to accept panic's visit when you really wish it would disappear.

The thing is, you have lots of practice accepting tough things already. Like when you read your favorite storybooks! As you turn the pages, you encounter scary characters, joyful scenes, plot twists, enormous challenges, victories, and of course dark, frightening moments.

You accept the full story by not skipping over the hard parts, avoiding scary pages, or rushing to the end of suspenseful chapters. You might **WANT** to only read the happy parts, but you know that's not what makes a good fairytale!

Well, your feelings, sensations, thoughts, and struggles are all parts of your life's story. Even the hard ones, like panic.

When panic shows up, keep noticing and allowing each part of your experience, like you're reading the scary parts of a story page by page. Don't close the book by pushing panic away. Don't try to change the storyline by letting panic change your actions. Trust that like every good fairy tale, panic will unfold and come to an end on its own, just like it always does.

Think of a time that you felt panic (it can be a long time
ago or yesterday), and create a storybook page about it.
What happened?

One thing I felt proud of was...

Remember, just like every story, every moment of panic has an end.

Finally, show your panic some **love**.

When panic shows up, your activating system is in overdrive, and you feel afraid. When you add anger and frustration into the mix, your panic thinks there's even more danger, and it grows bigger.

But if, when panic pops up, you treat it with love and kindness instead, you're telling your brain that there's nothing to be afraid of. Panic thinks it's not needed, so it starts to relax. The fear spell weakens.

The trick to loving panic, even though you don't like it, is to treat it like you would treat a good friend who is caring, but overprotective, impulsive, and a bit...misguided. Like a barking dog who thinks he's defending the house from the evil mailman, or thinks you need to be saved from the dangerous squirrels in the yard!

When Valentina's panic pops up before a sleepover, she imagines what she would say to her adorable but naughty dog Henry, who she loves, if he was trying to protect her from something that isn't dangerous.

Here are some things you might say to your panic from a place of love:

- Dear panic, I LOVE you. I know you're trying to help me.

- I'm sending kindness to my heart—it's racing and it must feel tired.

- Thank you lungs, I know you're doing the best you can to help me breathe.

- Dear body, thank you. You deserve a big hug when you tremble. I know you're scared.

- I feel compassion for my belly, it's feeling tangled up and doesn't know that I'm safe.

Can you think of two more?

1. ____

____

2. ____

____

Next time your panic shows up, send it some love and watch your fear relax a bit!

CHAPTER 6

The Power of Your Body

Panic is an expert at using your body's activating system to make you feel afraid. So one of the best ways to fight back with your own power is to become an expert at using your body's calming system. Makes sense right?

With practice, your sense of personal power will grow and you'll be able to stand your ground more easily when panic comes around.

Plus, learning to use your calming system can also help you:

► sleep better

► have less pain

► strengthen your immune system

► feel happier

► make stronger and more lasting memories

► have a healthy heart

► improve your relationships

► have more energy

► be more creative

► have more motivation

► make fear spells bounce off of you

Here are some fun ways to turn on your calming system, get your body back in balance, and leave your panic on shaky ground.

Magic Breathing

Magic breathing is slow, steady, and deep. It helps you calm your body down during tough moments and stay calmer in the first place.

When your body is panicked, your breathing is fast and shallow. When you're calm, you naturally breathe more deeply and slowly.

So what's magical about breathing like this? Taking relaxed breaths instantly turns on your body's calming system, without you even trying to calm down. Panic gets so confused. After all, why would your breath be so slow and steady if you were in danger?

▶ Breathe in slowly and deeply through your nose. Let your breath fill up your belly & chest. You can imagine you're inflating like a balloon!

▶ Hold your breath for a second, and then very slowly breathe out through your mouth like you are trying to gently cool down that mug of hot cocoa you made earlier without it spilling over.

▶ Try to **SLOW** your breathing way down. Aim for 6 seconds in and 6 seconds out.

▶ Try placing your hands on your belly and feeling it rise and fall with each breath you take.

▶ Now try placing your hands over your heart area and imagine your body softening and relaxing as you breathe.

Another way to do magic breathing is snake breath! Breathe in (slowly!) and when you breathe out, make a *sssss* sound like a snake.

Set a timer and practice breathing slowly and deeply for two minutes, then write or draw about how you feel. Do you feel different after?

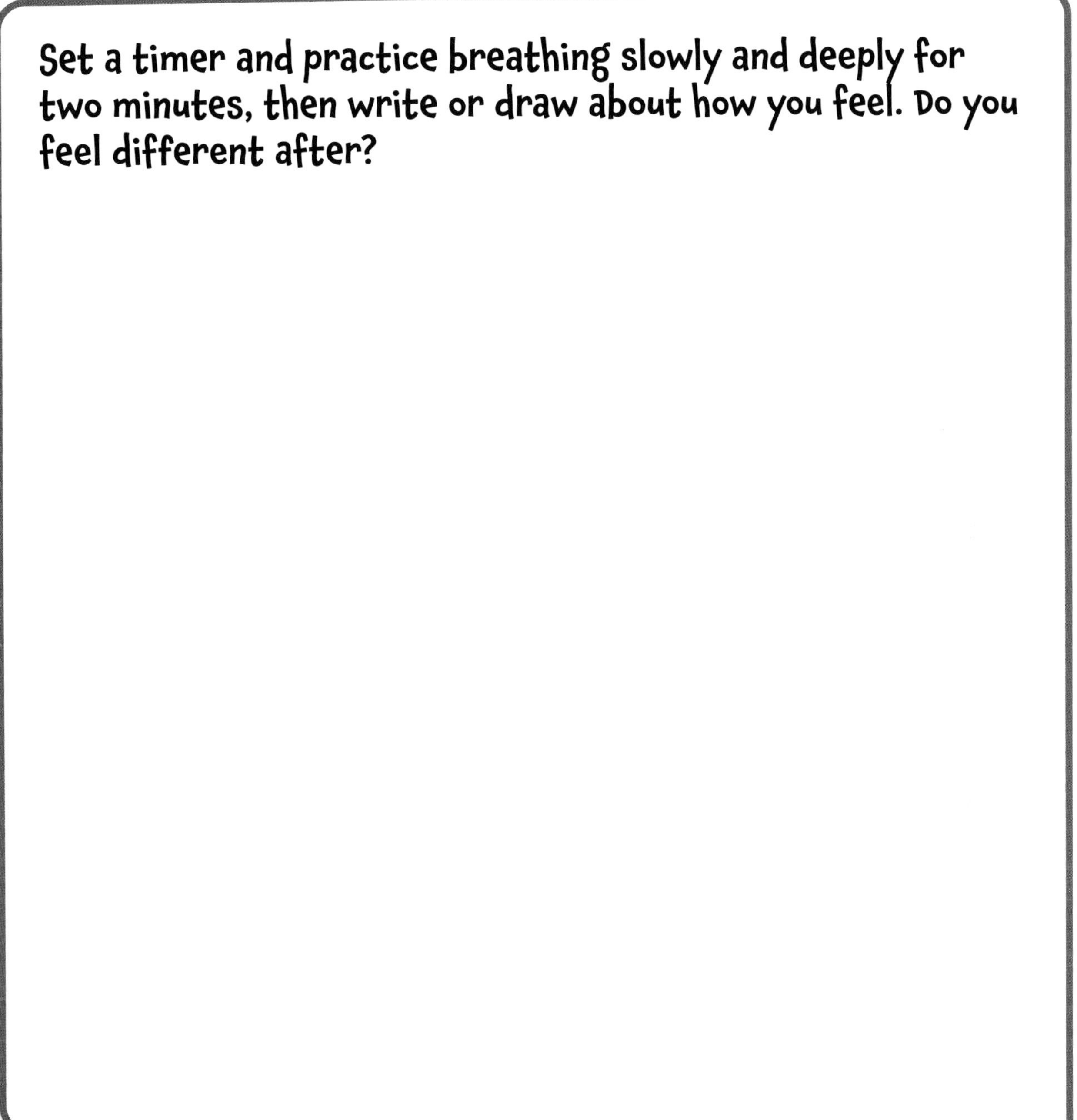

Try to practice magic breathing every day for a few minutes, and not just when you're panicking. Just like playing an instrument, or a sport, the more you practice, the easier it will get!

Magic Movement

Get moving! You already know that panic powers up your body so you can run, fight, or hide. So you need to take some of that power back into your own hands and use it to find your balance! There are lots of fun ways to move your body, like:

- jumping

- twirling

- dancing

- running up and down the stairs

- pressing and holding your hands up against a wall

- wiggling and shaking

- flying around your room on a pretend magic broomstick

By moving this way you're tricking panic into believing you're not afraid, even if you totally are. Who dances in the face of danger? Once panic thinks it's not scaring you, it backs off.

As a bonus, it's empowering to learn that you're in charge of your body, and can make it move however you want, even when panic makes you think you're frozen in place.

Choose one of the movements above, set a timer, and go all out for 1-2 minutes. What was that like?

The next time your panic shows up, try moving that same way. See what happens!

Did your panic fade faster?   ☐ yes   ☐ no

Did you feel stronger and more in
    charge of your body?   ☐ yes   ☐ no

Did it surprise you that you could move this
    way even in the middle of panic?   ☐ yes   ☐ no

Magic Energy

Deep within each of us lies a special kind of energy that's uniquely our own. Some call it their "spirit," their "spark," or their inner "light." No matter what you call it, your inner energy is always with you, flowing through your body, even when you're scared.

Panic has its own energy too, and it washes over your body like waves of fear. The incredible thing is, you can use your inner energy to transform panic and how it makes you feel.

Picture your special inner energy. What does it look like? Does it have a shape? A color? Is it still or moving?

Emma imagined hers as a fluttering butterfly in her body's center, while Sam pictured a glowing ball that shined light throughout his body. Valentina envisioned hers like a sparkling stream, carrying shimmer to wherever it was needed.

Draw your own inner energy, just how you imagine it. You can draw it inside of your body, or separately.

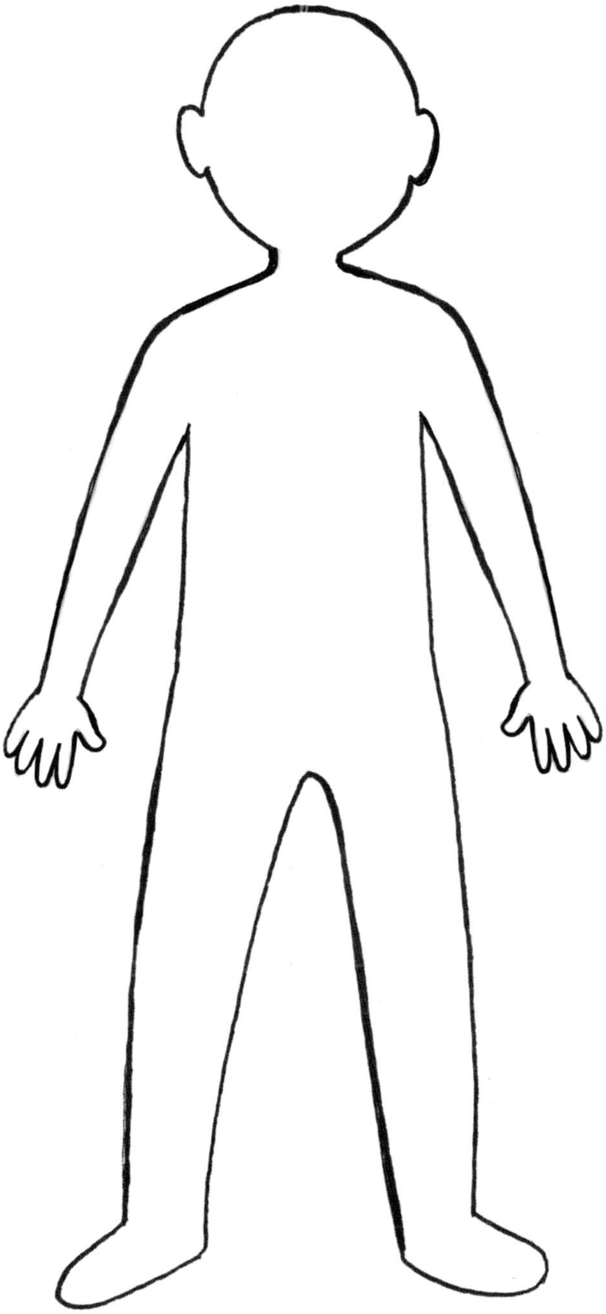

Finding and using your inner energy might be new to you, but it will feel natural and easy once you get the hang of it.

Bring your hands together in front of your chest, gently (but firmly) pressing your palms against each other. Keep your back tall and straight, and raise your elbows up slightly. Close your eyes, and take a few deep breaths. Find your stillness. Can you feel the power pulsing between your hands? Maybe you feel a bit of warmth or tingling through your fingers and arms? Do you hear your heart beating? That's your inner energy!

The next time panic tries to overwhelm you, find your inner energy, and **IMAGINE** moving **TOWARDS** panic instead of away from it. Allow yourself to lean **INTO** panic's energy instead of resisting it. Think of diving right through panic's waves instead of bracing for impact.

Have you ever gotten into a chilly pool? You have to jump into the cold water (or walk in slowly if that's more your style) before the water can feel warm. You must go towards the cold before you can get comfortable. That's exactly how it feels to move towards your panic.

You don't actually have to move your body at all. The movement is happening within you, on an energetic level. You could be using your inner energy to melt away your panic in the middle of class, and no-one looking at you would even notice a thing! It's like creating your very own illusion.

CHAPTER 7

The Power of Your Mind

Did you know that your brain comes up with about 70,000 thoughts each day? And that your thoughts are instantly connected to your feelings, memories, skills, and even how you feel about yourself? Incredible!

Think of the thoughts in your mind like stars in the sky, that's how many there are! Some are neutral, some are positive, and some are scary, but from a distance, they all sort of....look similar.

I think there's chewing gum on my shoe—gross.
I everyone staring at me?
What if school got taken over by aliens?
I wonder what Emma's doing.
I like my shoes.
Math.... ugh.
What if everyone is staring at me because I have spinach in my teeth?
What if I get sick and miss the big game?
I'm glad it's Friday!
Where did dinosaurs sleep?
It's warm today.
What if something bad happens?
Is blue raspberry a real thing?

Positive, brave thoughts feed your confidence and make it stronger, while negative, fearful thoughts fuel your panic and make it grow bigger.

You can't stop your mind from creating panicky thoughts, but you CAN train your brain to create more brave, positive thoughts, which will help you feel much more balanced and courageous.

The tricky thing is, your mind is designed to pay more attention to negative, fearful thoughts. It can feel like they are bigger or louder.

You can't make those negative thoughts disappear but you **CAN** change how you notice them, which will make even your scariest thoughts seem just like any other ordinary thoughts—barely noticeable.

Emma stood backstage waiting to perform a dance routine she'd been working on for months and felt her stomach get tight. Suddenly her mind was racing with scary thoughts like:

Before she knew it, she was in panic mode.

Does your mind ever sound like that? That's called negative self-talk, and it makes you feel less confident. And you already know that panic grows bigger when you feel small.

Write down some negative thoughts that run through your mind when you're panicking. You can even include some comments that you imagine would make your panic worse.

To be free from panic, you need to learn to talk to yourself in a **positive,** helpful way instead. The more you practice creating, reading, and rehearsing positive self-talk, the faster your brain will learn to do this on its own.

Emma had been practicing her positive self-talk and was totally ready! She paused, took a deep breath, and said to herself:

It worked just like magic! Her fear eased just enough to help give her the confidence to go out there.

A powerful trick that helped Emma find the right words so easily was to picture her thoughts as book titles in a magic library. Take a look at some of her favorites:

Your turn!

Read your statements over and over until they feel easy to remember. Try speaking to yourself this way the next time you panic, or before facing something that makes you nervous.

Another great way to train your brain to think courageous thoughts more easily is to take on the fearless energy of your favorite athlete, superhero, or fairy tale character and practice talking to yourself in their voice. This will give you some of their confidence that you can keep for yourself.

Valentina's parents needed to attend back-to-school night, leaving her older sister to babysit. Right away, Valentina noticed a lot of scary thoughts, like "What if something bad happens while they're gone? What if something goes wrong and we can't reach them? What if I panic and can't calm down?"

Valentina thought of her favorite superhero. She imagined herself putting on a magic hat that gave her the power to see his innermost thoughts and feel his courage. She pictured him in a situation where he felt panic and imagined what he would be saying to himself:

► "I can do this! I'm stronger than I feel right now, I just know it."

► "I've faced lots of challenges, and this one is no different."

► "I have to at least try."

► "I'm panicking, but I won't let that stop me."

Valentina chuckled a bit, because the idea of this powerful character being scared or saying words like "panicking" sounded silly. She noticed her panic getting lighter, and felt encouraged to keep coming up with some brave thoughts of her own. "I'm safe, and I'm not falling for panic's tricks this time," she thought.

Who's your favorite character, wizard, or your bravest friend? Imagine having a magic hat that allows you to think and feel things just like they do. What are three things they might say to themselves?

One fun (really!) way to change your relationship with your panic thoughts is to turn your scariest thoughts into…a song! This helps you notice these thoughts as just thoughts, instead of feeling overwhelmed by them. It's like seeing a scary werewolf in a movie; you see him snarling, but you're not in the movie with him.

► Write down your worst, scariest panic thought or two—the ones that bring up the most fear.

► Think of the melody for "Twinkle, Twinkle Little Star."

► Then match your panic thoughts to the rhythm of the song.

Here is an example that Sam wrote—sing his words out loud to the tune.

Your turn! Take your own lyrics and sing them to the melody. You can use any panic thoughts you want, and any song you want! You can even write your own rap verse, if you have that talent. Go all out!

Now sing it over and over again until the panic words seem just like... words. You might even notice yourself feeling bored instead of scared. Even better? These scary thoughts might sound so silly that they make you laugh. Fear is transformed!

CHAPTER 8

The Power of Your Actions

Imagine an enchanted bridge connecting two lands: one full of shadows and storms, where **panic rules** and darkness surrounds you. And on the other side, a land full of light, confidence, and adventure, where **you** are in charge. You'd cross the bridge to the light side right away right? Except, below the bridge is a never-ending black hole swirling with uncertainty. Each time you try to

get across, you face strong gusts of doubt and fear that panic uses to pull you back.

Taking charge of your actions and doing what scares you feels just like that. But don't despair! The tricks and skills in this chapter will make your journey to confidence much easier.

Panic's ultimate goal is to keep you tucked into bed, hiding from the world, and not doing a single thing that might make you uncomfortable. No school, no practice, no team, no plane ride. And definitely **NO** trying the strategies in this book. That might feel really safe to you!

The problem is, if you avoid the hard stuff, you also miss out on all of the good stuff! Friends? That theme park trip with your family? Telling silly stories at a sleepover? Jumping off that diving board?

What's something that panic has stopped you from doing even though it wasn't actually dangerous?

To get back your personal power and crush panic's ability to stop you, you have to prove to yourself and to your panic that you don't need its protection. That you'll be ok on the other side!

But you can't just **TELL** panic to back off—you also have to **SHOW** it that the situation is safe, and that you are strong.

Facing your fears, and doing the things you love, over and over, makes that happen.

That's because you **LEARN** that:

► The more you do things that scare you, the easier they feel.

► Panic's worst predictions don't happen (or their chances of happening are teeny-tiny).

► You're stronger than you think and can get through hard things.

Bottom line? **You'll start to trust panic less and yourself more.**

Let's go!

Do the Opposite

This action strategy is simple: whatever panic is pulling you to do... do the opposite.

On the first day of school, Sam's new teacher asked for his name. He felt frozen in place, like he couldn't get the words out. Panic growled at him: "stay quiet and keep looking down!"

Instead, Sam looked up, said hello, and introduced himself loud and proud. Within minutes, his panic faded, and by lunch time he had forgotten it ever showed up.

First, let's practice pushing through a mini version of the discomfort that comes with doing the opposite. You'll feel more ready to overcome panic when you know what to expect.

What are you doing at this very moment? Eating a snack? Sitting? Focusing on this book?

Wherever you are, stand up tall, close your eyes and imagine you're standing on the very edge of an extra high diving board. Really let your mind go there! Then say to yourself (or out loud): **"Get ready. Get set. Go!"** And take a big leap forward.

What was that like? Maybe a little uncomfortable? Doing the opposite of what Panic wants may feel more intense, but it's the same type of sensation.

If you've ever jumped off of a high diving board, you know how scary it can be, but also how instantly the fear disappears once you're in the water.

Now see if you can pick the best way to practice doing the opposite in these panicky situations:

► If panic is telling you to not get on the bus to school:

- [ ] run to it excitedly and find your seat
- [ ] ask your parent for a ride to school
- [ ] give in and stay home
- [ ] take a really long time to get ready, so you can miss the bus pick up

► If panic is telling you to avoid speaking in class:

- [ ] stay in the back of the classroom so you don't get called on
- [ ] raise your hand as soon as you can and volunteer an answer
- [ ] ask to go to the bathroom
- [ ] doodle in your notebook

► If panic is telling you to hide away from your friends (who are friendly and safe, but you haven't seen them all summer):

- [ ] run up to them and give them a big hug
- [ ] excitedly call out to them and say hello
- [ ] walk up to them slowly, and smile
- [ ] any of the above

► If panic is telling you not to try out for the swim team (that your friends will all be on) because doing something new is always embarrassing:

- [ ] reassure yourself that it's ok not to do a sport this year
- [ ] tell your friends you'll be there, and then pretend you're sick & don't show up
- [ ] focus on your piano lessons and give up on your dreams to be a good swimmer
- [ ] none of the above

► You want to be in the school play, but your panic tells you that you can't handle the pressure that comes along with putting on a show.

- [ ] Ask to join the tech back-stage so that you get to at least be a part of the process
- [ ] Audition for the lead role
- [ ] Audition for the smallest part
- [ ] Ask a friend to go with you to the auditions so that you feel more courageous
- [ ] Any of the above

Now try matching a good opposite action to each of these common panic moments:

You are at a sleepover with a close friend when panic comes along and tells you to call home and ask to be picked up.

Jump up and march proudly into the exam room as soon as it's time.

You're at the doctor's office waiting to get called back, and panic is dragging you out the door.

Stay, eat some cake, and start a conversation with someone.

You're about to go out on stage for your first solo, when panic tells you you can't do it.

Raise your hand straight up and ask a question in your most confident voice.

You're at a friend's birthday party and you feel embarrassed about making a joke nobody laughed at. Panic is telling you to go home early.

Go out there and give it your best try.

Panic tells you not to raise your hand to ask a question in science in case your teacher thinks your question is silly.

Give your friend a hug, and commit to staying all night.

Choose a panicky situation where you could practice "doing the opposite."

Draw or write about what **panic wants** you to do:	Draw or write what **you could** do instead:

Do What You Love (Even When It Feels Scary)

Another great panic-defeating action is to just...do the things you love. Instead of only going **AGAINST** what panic wants, go **TOWARDS** things that make you feel a sense of pride and joy.

The goal is for you to live your best life and be the kid you want to be, as if panic wasn't there. Think of panic like a little bug sitting on your shoulder (no offense to bugs, the earth needs them!). Let it come along with you while you get busy doing things that you love.

Remember, panic isn't powerful unless you feel afraid. It's hard to feel afraid when you feel good, right? The magic of this strategy is that you aren't even battling panic, you aren't paying attention to it at all, you're just doing your own thing.

► Emma kept showing up at dance, because she really loved it, even though sometimes performing made her panic.

► Valentina kept making sleepover plans, even though being away from home was really hard. Her friends were the best, and she didn't want to miss out!

► Sam signed up for music camp, even though he knew his panic might show up. Making progress was important to him, and made him feel good about himself.

The Land of

_______'s

____
(Fill in your name)

Best Life.

One thing that I love doing is... ___________

____

Two activities that make me feel accomplished are... ___________

____

I want to be the type of friend who... ___________

____

One person I feel close to is... ___________

____

The thing I value most in a friend is... ___________

____

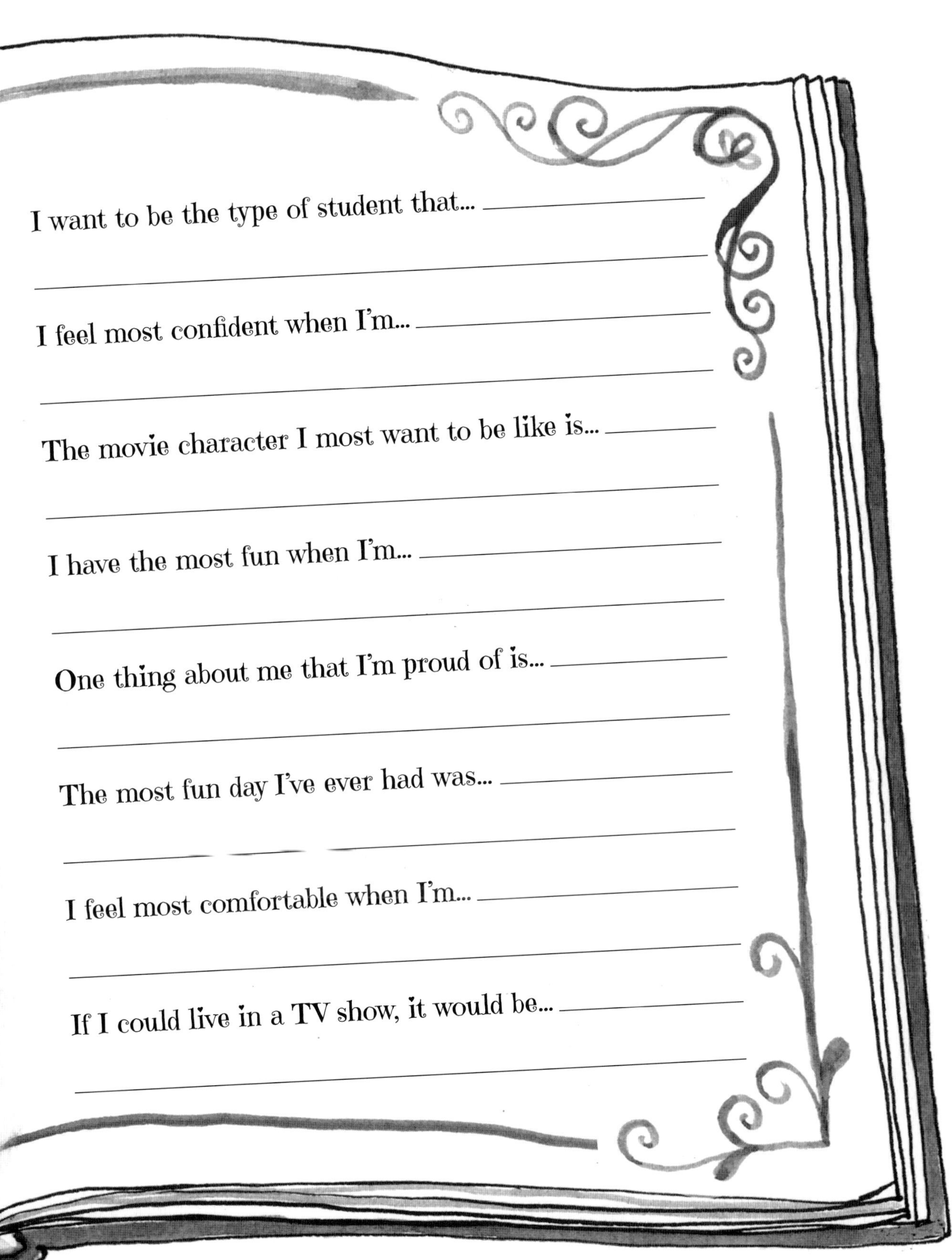

I want to be the type of student that...

I feel most confident when I'm...

The movie character I most want to be like is...

I have the most fun when I'm...

One thing about me that I'm proud of is...

The most fun day I've ever had was...

I feel most comfortable when I'm...

If I could live in a TV show, it would be...

Use what you've learned about yourself and make a list of some things you love that would make your life better. Bonus points for listing things that panic has stopped you from doing lately.

Share your list with a parent, and talk to them about how they could help you do more of these things more often.

Panic might still pop up every now and then and try to scare you out of taking charge of your actions. Be ready to push through these feelings by reminding yourself why it's worth it.

Untangling a Panic Web

Like a black cat and bad luck, panic and uncomfortable body sensations go hand in hand. When you panic, your activating system instantly causes sensations like a fast heartbeat, queasiness, or shakiness. Because this feels so intense, your brain forms a strong memory linking these sensations to fear (without you even knowing it!).

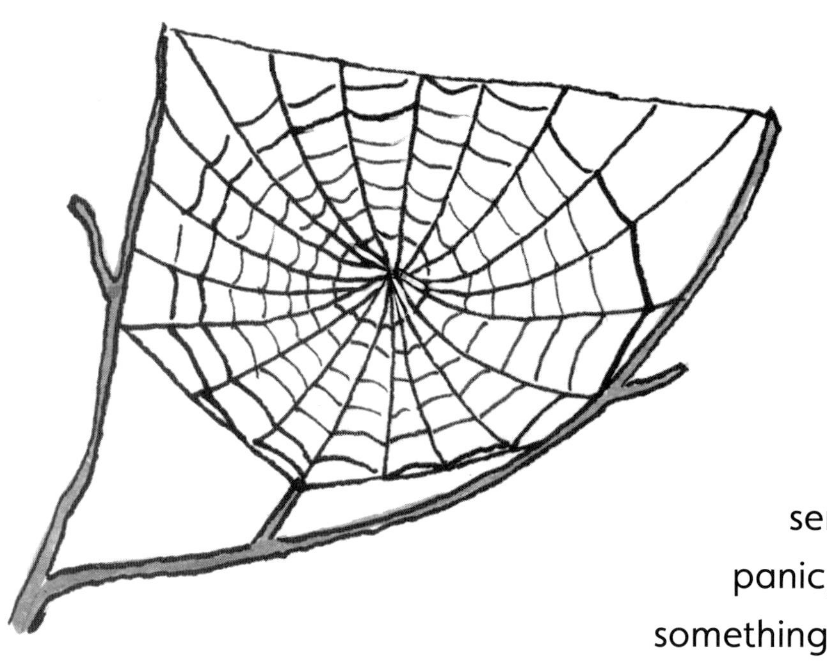

For kids who struggle with panic, these sensations can become connected to fear, even though they aren't dangerous.

Next thing you know, these sensations can cause you to panic, even when they start from something totally separate.

Even something exciting, like sprinting after a soccer ball, or totally ordinary, like your belly feeling grumbly in the morning, can now make you panic! And of course, your panic then makes those sensations even worse. It becomes a tangled web of panic and fear.

If this happens to you, the fastest way to throw panic off balance is to reverse the connections your mind made, and disrupt this cycle. That means creating panicky sensations in your body on purpose, for short periods of time, and sitting with them until they pass.

Why? When you practice these sensations over and over, without anything awful happening, your brain learns that they don't automatically mean danger. It loosens the connection.

The panicky sensations start to feel less scary as you get used to them, **AND** your mind starts to connect them with a sense of safety instead of fear. Without fear, panic has zero power—it can't even begin to cast a good fear spell!

When you untangle fear from physical sensations, your mind learns:

► Feeling a bit of dizziness does NOT mean I'm unsafe.

► Feeling hot and tingly does NOT mean something bad is about to happen.

► An "off" feeling in my belly does NOT mean I'll throw up everywhere.

► A black cat does NOT mean bad luck (at least not always!).

It's like finding out that sometimes a black cat can mean good luck instead.

Over time, panic gets out of the habit of showing up at the wrong time and place, and starts to realize that an uncomfortable sensation in your body can even mean...nothing at all.

You might want to practice this strategy with a trusted adult by your side (at least the first time). You can even ask them to DO it with you.

Step 1. Pick a few sensations that come with your panic from the list below and practice making them happen in your body.

If you start to feel panicky...great! Your goal is to get used to the sensations.

If you don't feel much? Try upping the intensity—really get into it (it can feel awkward to go all out at first); or try doing the strategies for a bit longer.

Shallow breathing	Make your breathing short and quick for 60 seconds, on purpose, while standing
Tightness in your throat	Swallow quickly 10 times in a row.
Heart pounding	Run quickly in place or do fast jumping jacks for 60 seconds.
Queasiness	Spin in a swivel chair or twirl on your feet as fast as you can. Start with a few spins and work your way up to 30 seconds.
Dizziness	Shake your head side to side quickly, with your eyes open for 30 seconds.
Lightheadedness	Hold your breath for 15-20 seconds.

Step 2. Notice your panic (and body sensations). Let it be there. Sit with it, let it stay with you.

► Get curious about the sensations and don't try to make them go away.

► Try to notice your panic like an observer, without jumping into it.

► Watch how the panicky feelings rise, fall, and dissolve on their own.

Step 3. Help your mind put it all together by checking the answers that fit best.

► I realized that my panic is…

- ☐ More powerful than I thought
- ☐ Less powerful than I thought

► Did my biggest fear come true?

- ☐ Yes
- ☐ No
- ☐ Partially

► How do I feel about myself?

- ☐ Good
- ☐ Bad
- ☐ Neutral
- ☐ Proud

► I learned that I'm able to handle discomfort:

- ☐ Better than I expected
- ☐ Worse than I expected
- ☐ Not at all, even for a second

Practice over and over (aim for at least once per day) and watch as your fear disappears!

CHAPTER 10

A Dose of Self-Love

We already talked about showing your panic love...but YOU need some self-love to be free from panic, too.

You can use self-love to instantly feel better when you're panicked. But even more power lies in practicing self-love regularly, because the better you feel about yourself, the less likely panic is to show up in the first place.

Think of self-love like the light of a magic candle that sits in your window, signaling to panic that it's not needed. The soft flame is the ultimate protection against fear spells!

When you feel anger, guilt, and frustration with yourself, your activating

system turns on, and your panic gets bigger. When you feel kindness and self-compassion, your calming system turns on instead and your panic gets smaller.

Panic knows it isn't needed right then and there. Your brain is not designed to be afraid in the face of loving feelings. Makes sense right?

By practicing daily, your self-love candle stays lit, and creates a magical shield all around you. Like a protection charm!

Create Feelings of Self-Love

The fastest way to build self-love is to feel it in your body. Making feelings appear in your body might be a new skill for you, but once you learn it, it's easy.

► Find a comfortable place and position to sit down.

► Notice any wiggles, jiggles, or tensions that your body is holding on to. Let them out if you need to.

► Now relax your body.

► Place your right hand over your heart and close your eyes.

► Take a few slow, long, deep breaths.

► Imagine warmth and kindness flowing from your hand straight to your heart.

► Stay with that feeling. Let yourself really take it in.

► Now imagine this energy flowing through the rest of your body, like sunshine covering you in a warm comforting glow.

► Stay with that feeling. Really take it in.

► Open your eyes. Take a few more relaxed breaths.

Were you able to notice feelings of love and warmth? It's almost impossible to feel this sensation and fear at the same time. Your panic simply can't get through the magic shield.

Take a few minutes every day to practice this, and watch your self-love glow brighter.

Find Your Most Loving Voice

When you talk to yourself with compassion and kindness, your self-love grows (as does your courage and resilience!). Sometimes it's hard to think of what to say and find your most loving voice, especially when you're feeling panicked or down.

Creating a jar full of supportive statements that you can read each day will help you practice self-love more easily.

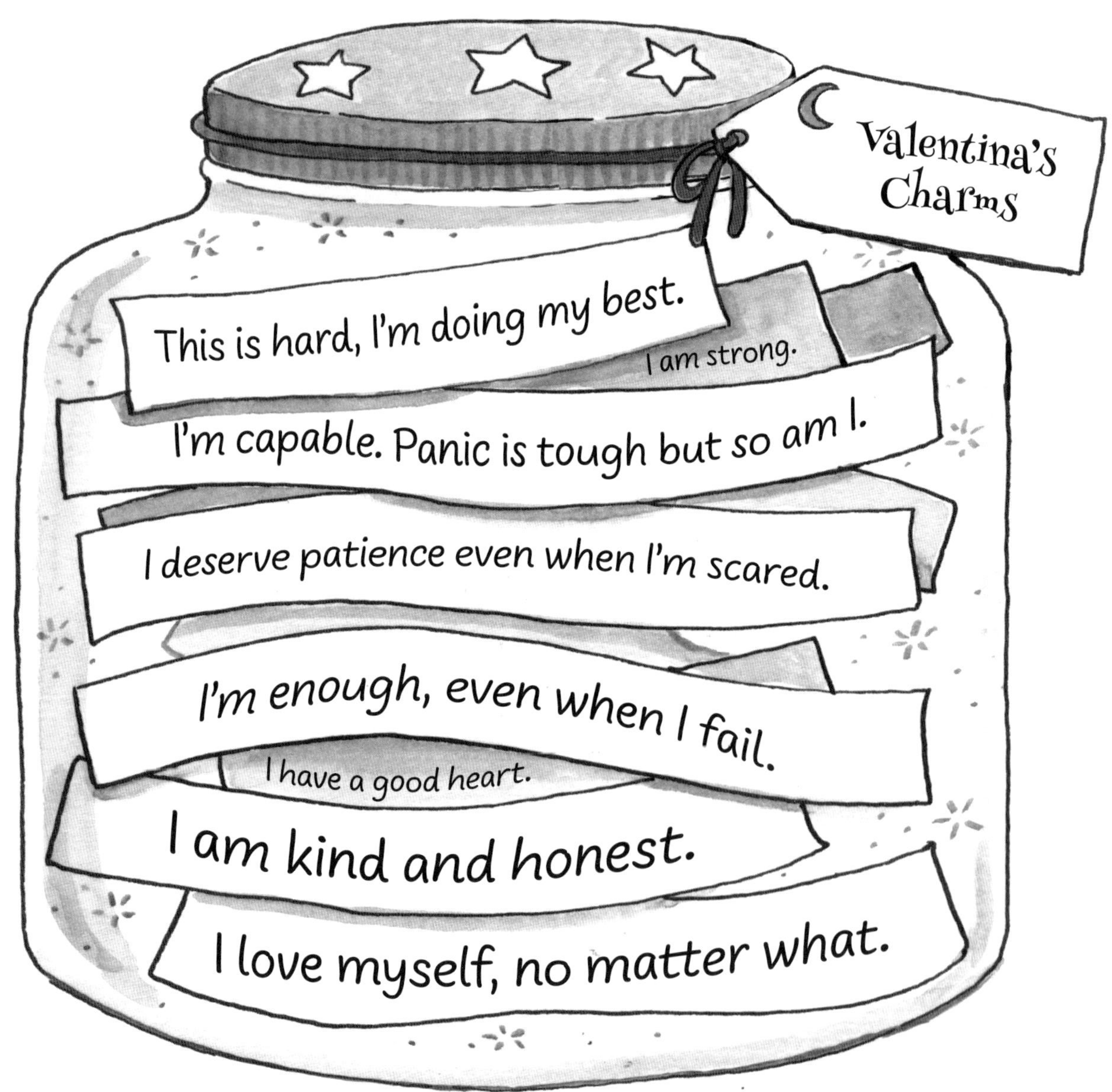

Your turn!

Create your own magic jar and fill it up with kind, compassionate statements. You can use some of Valentina's loving words to help you get started. Just change them up to make sure they feel true to **you**.

You may not believe the words at first, but over time, your loving voice will feel fully yours. That's the power of self-love!

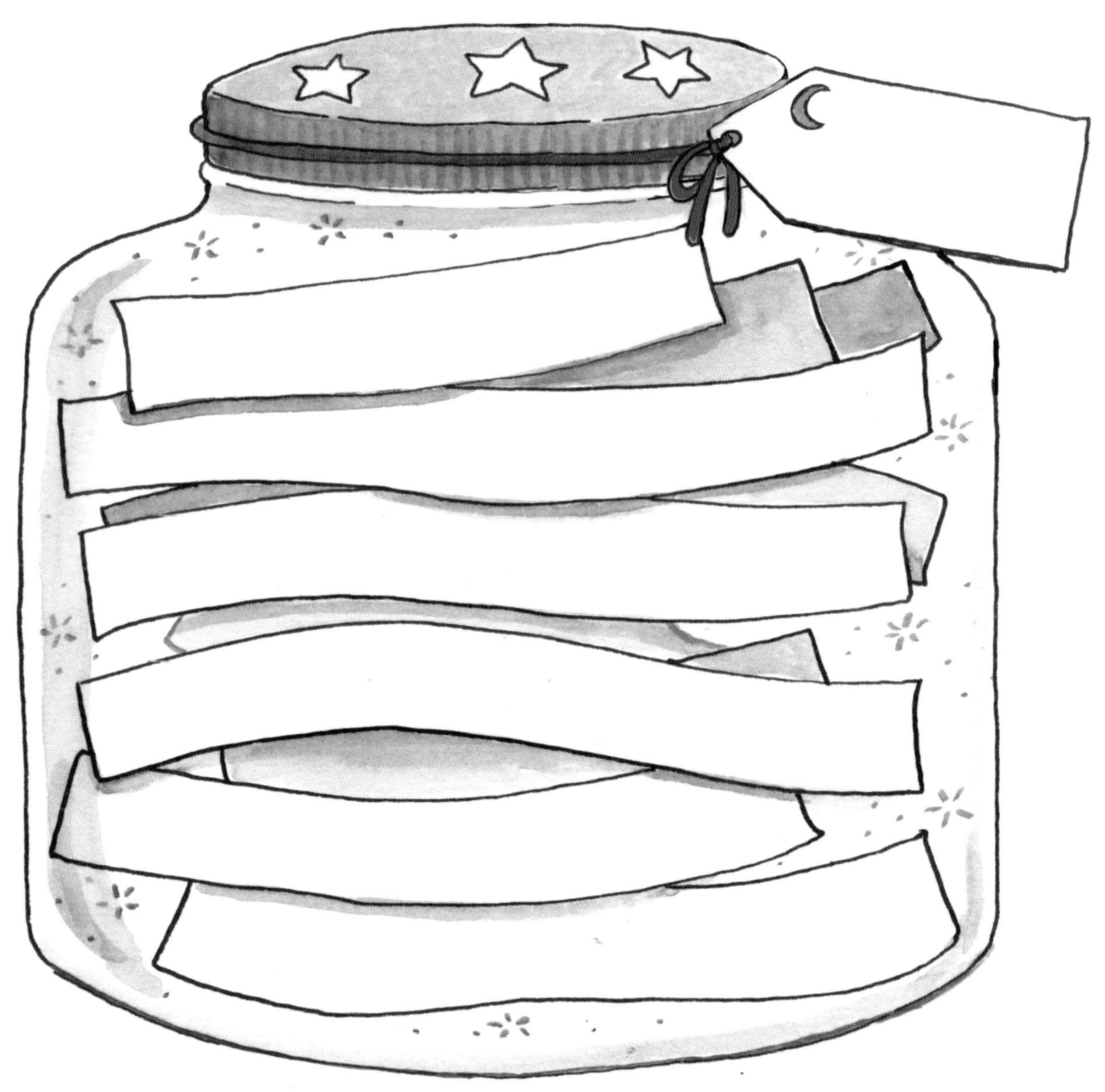

CHAPTER 11

You Did It!

You made it! I hope you feel so proud of yourself. You have transformed your relationship with panic, page by page. This shows just how STRONG you are. Panic is tricky, but it's no match for the power that lies within YOU. If you keep practicing what you've learned, your fear of panic will continue to get smaller, your confidence will grow bigger, and doing the things you love will feel a lot easier.

Remember:

► Your fear of panic is what makes it grow.

► Avoiding, running from, or getting mad at panic make it stronger.

► Connect with your inner energy and move towards panic to weaken its power.

► Welcome panic with curiosity and kindness to break the fear spell it has over you.

► Your body, mind, and actions are the keys to your personal power. Take charge of them.

► You and your panic both deserve love. No matter what.

► Be true to yourself, and do what brings you joy and pride. Panic is an afterthought.

Staying untangled from panic takes time, practice, and effort, but it's SO worth it.

ABOUT THE AUTHOR

Lenka Glassman, PsyD, is a licensed psychologist specializing in the treatment of anxiety and related conditions. She works with children, teens, adults, and families on issues related to anxiety, obsessive-compulsive disorder, and self-esteem.

ABOUT THE ILLUSTRATOR

Janet McDonnell's illustrations combine traditional media and digital techniques. In addition to illustrating books, magazines, and puzzles, Janet has both taught and written for children from preschool to high school ages.

MAGINATION PRESS

The American Psychological Association works to advance psychology as a science and profession, as a means to improve health and human welfare. APA publishes books for young readers under its imprint, Magination Press. It's the combined power of psychology and literature that helps kids navigate life's challenges more easily. Visit maginationpress.org and @MaginationPress on Facebook, X, Instagram, and Pinterest.